In memory of
Stella (Stelle)
Stephanie Czopor,
mother of Carol Brackeen and
Ed Czopor Jr.
This book is a tribute to her
special love of reading, sincere
involvement and genuine respect
for young children.
Donated to
the Children's Workshop

Collection by Heather Bakas

Date April 7, 1999

STILL

by
Karen E. Lotz

illustrated by
Colleen Browning

DUTTON CHILDREN'S BOOKS
NEW YORK

Library of Congress Cataloging-in-Publication Data

Lotz, Karen E.
Can't sit still / by Karen E. Lotz; illustrated by Colleen Browning.—1st ed.
p. cm.
Summary: A child observes the changing sights and sounds of each
new season in the city.
ISBN 0-525-45066-1
[1. Seasons—Fiction.   2. City and town life—Fiction.]
I. Browning, Colleen, ill.   II. Title.   92-28853
PZ7.L9195Can   1993   CIP   [E]—dc20   AC

Published in the United States 1993 by Dutton Children's Books,
a division of Penguin Books USA Inc.
375 Hudson Street, New York, New York 10014

Designed by Barbara Powderly

Printed in Hong Kong   First Edition
10 9 8 7 6 5 4 3 2 1

The illustrations for this book were painted in watercolor on
heavy paper primed with acrylic gesso and stretched individually
on frames like canvas. Some areas of watercolor were sanded;
felt pens, colored pencils, and pastels were also used.

autumn in the city

pump the pedals

race the sun

   slipping

      sliding

down the block

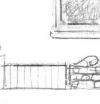

wind smells like hot java beans

tickles the hairs on the back of my neck

cats mess around in the trash next door

momma calls

get in here and eat

squeak the rubber

to a stop

lock it up

for after supper

momma says baby you going to
catch cold on those floors

wiggle my toes so they don't stick together
don't need shoes when you can't sit still

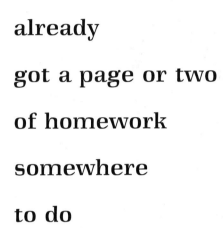

already

got a page or two

of homework

somewhere

to do

winter in the city

hop

    skiddle

        glide

on the too cold floor

run the faucets

hot and steamy

paint my name in magic ink

momma says what you been

growing in those ears

soap slips

down to my lips

sputter   sputter   spit

climb all clean into grandma's patchwork tent

storm wants to sleep over

slinks between the buildings

black mice hide in the pantry

mister cat says excuse me

but I'll be asking you to leave

momma calls better pull out

your long underwear tomorrow

can't hear a thing

making my marks

a silent animal

stepping in the snow

somebody in heaven's having a pillow fight

no recess today

school's closing early

can't sit still

spring in the city

pack mister cat

on my back

slip out the window and up the ladder

air on the roof is fresh and good

scribble on the park

with my tree-green crayon

make the red car

stop and go

fat black tire bellies slick up the rain

lightning strikes

in mister cat's fur

momma calls

you up there child well get down right now

jump two

bump two

drag the bag

four flights of steps

tomorrow's garbage day

momma says

here you go baby

you forgot the tuna

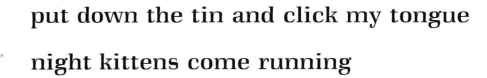

put down the tin and click my tongue

night kittens come running

listen to their tiny mouths

nibble nibble

smack   smack   smack

summer in the city

skip cracks up the block

left foot only

right foot on the way back

lick the sticky sweet from my hand

momma says why thank you baby

just what I needed

big sister stoop-sitting

with a boy and a box

music splashes on the neighbor's van

mister cat heads down cellar for cool

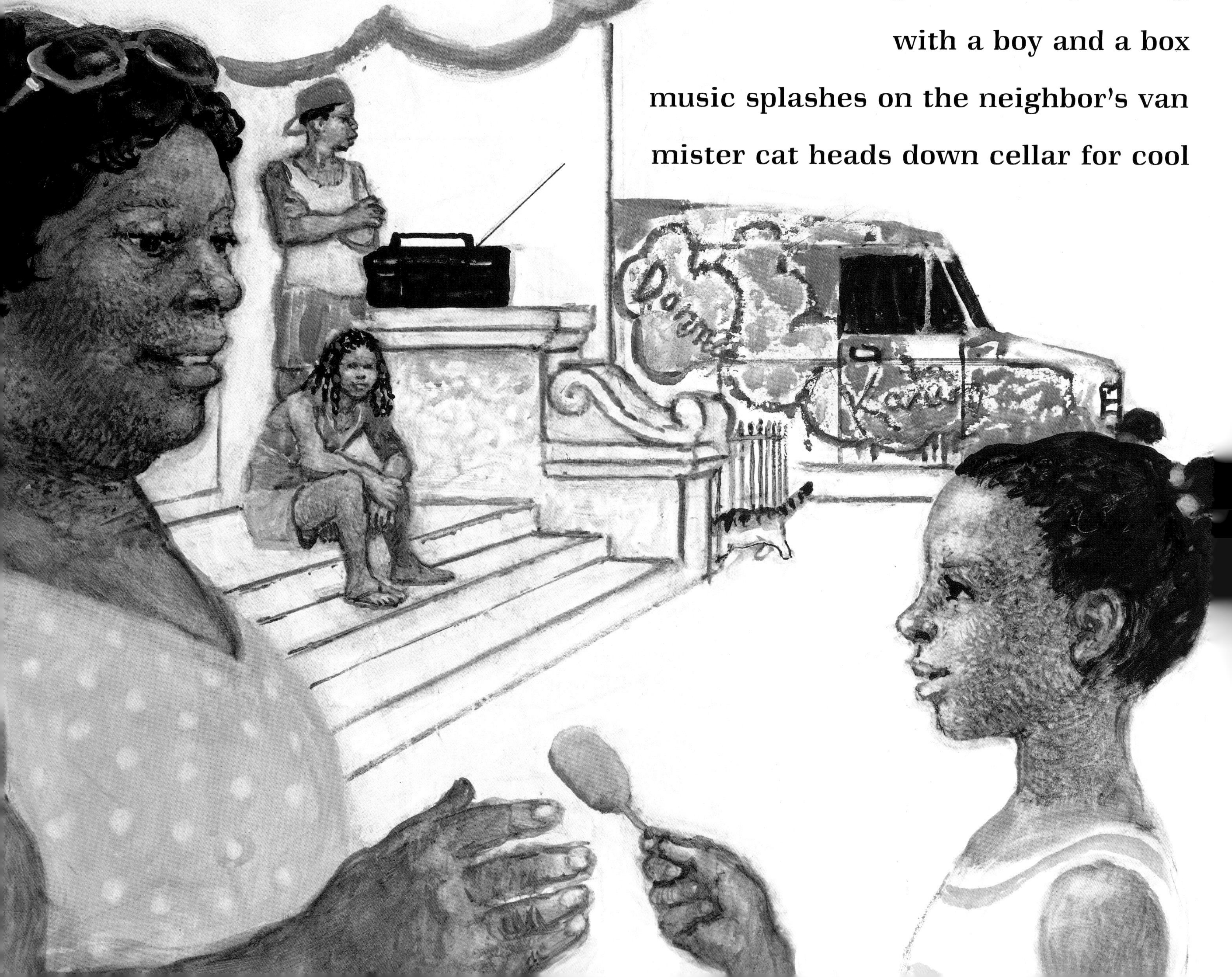

hanging in the laundromat

skin glistens shiny brown

can't sit still

turn

fly

spin

dry

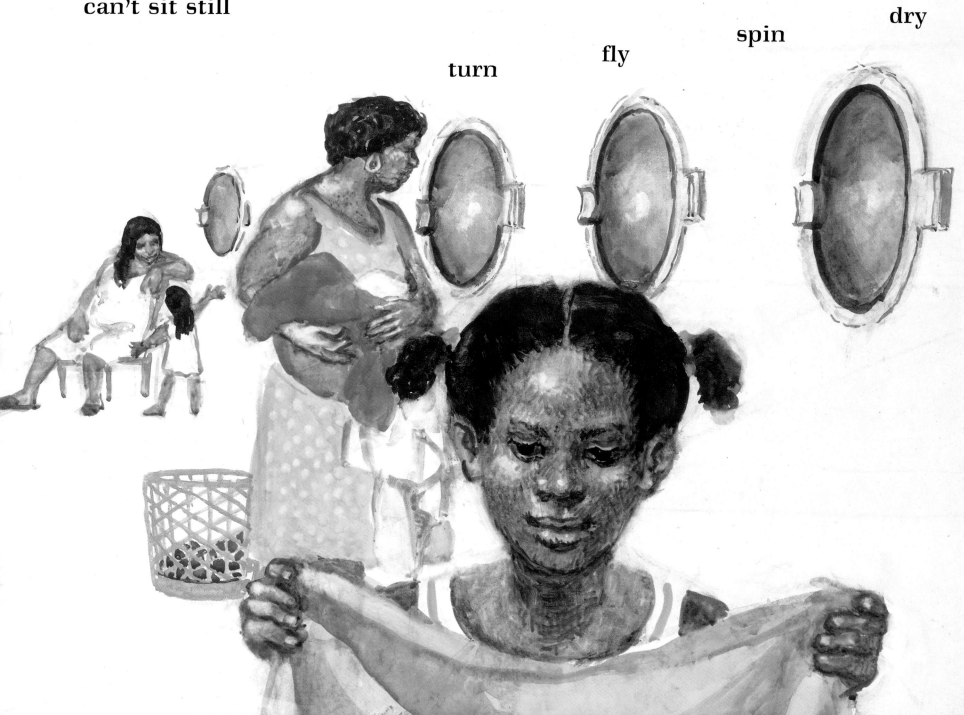

momma calls

better hurry back outside baby

if you want to ride on Old Eli

give the man my quarter

let the air take me up

ride the night

home.

about the author and illustrator

Born in New Mexico and raised in South Carolina and Virginia, KAREN E. LOTZ always enjoyed books about big cities when she was a child. She finally got a firsthand taste of city living at college in Cambridge, Massachusetts, where she studied poetry and literature. Later, her knowledge of urban culture grew when she volunteered for a year as a family-crisis counselor in the heart of Washington, D.C. But it wasn't until she moved to Brooklyn that the musical rhythms and hubbub of New York, imagined in childhood daydreams, truly came to life. The author, a children's book editor and an oboist, also enjoys traveling, most recently to the remote rain forest of equatorial Africa—where she discovered a very different kind of populous, bustling civilization.

COLLEEN BROWNING is an internationally renowned realist painter acclaimed for her mastery of the human figure as well as for her discoveries of shape and pattern in the commonplace. Her work is in the public collections of major museums across the country and has been the subject of articles in *The New York Times, Time* and *Newsweek* magazines, and other periodicals. An Academician of the National Academy of Design and the recipient of a number of prestigious awards, Colleen Browning has taught painting at various institutions and is the author of *Working Out a Painting*. She lived for many years in East Harlem when she first came to the United States from Ireland. She now divides her time between New York City and Grenada.